SEA WITCHES

SEA WITCHES

by
Joanne Robertson

illustrated by
Laszlo Gal

Dial Books for Young Readers · New York

First published in the United States 1991 by
Dial Books for Young Readers
A Division of Penguin Books USA Inc.
375 Hudson Street · New York, New York 10014

Published in Canada by
Oxford University Press, Ontario, Canada.
Text copyright © 1991 by Joanne Robertson
Pictures copyright © 1991 by Laszlo Gal
Printed in Hong Kong
First Edition
1 3 5 7 9 10 8 6 4 2

Library of Congress Cataloging in Publication Data
Robertson, Joanne.
Sea Witches/by Joanne Robertson: pictures by Laszlo Gal.
p. cm.
Summary: A Scottish grandmother explains the legend
behind an old superstition to her grandson:
Always crumble your eggshells, else the sea witches
will get them and turn them into boats, from which
they will cause storms and shipwrecks on the oceans.
ISBN 0-8037-1070-4
[1. Folklore—Scotland.] I. Gal, Laszlo, ill. II. Title.
PZ8.1.R54Se 1992   398.2—dc20   [E]   91-233   CIP   AC

To Richard, with love
–J.R.

To Phyllis Fogelman
–L.G.

With this weird warning
My Scottish grandmother served
Soft-boiled eggs for lunch:

"When you're done eating,
Give your eggshells a beating!
Never leave them whole!"

"Why?" I would ask her,
While into sharp jagged shards
I shattered the shells.

This story she told:
"Ghastly ghost witches gather
In the darkling gloom.

Silently they come,
Broom-riding, hideous hags,
In search of eggshells.

Down to earth they steal,
Weaving eerie, evil spells
And gathering shells.

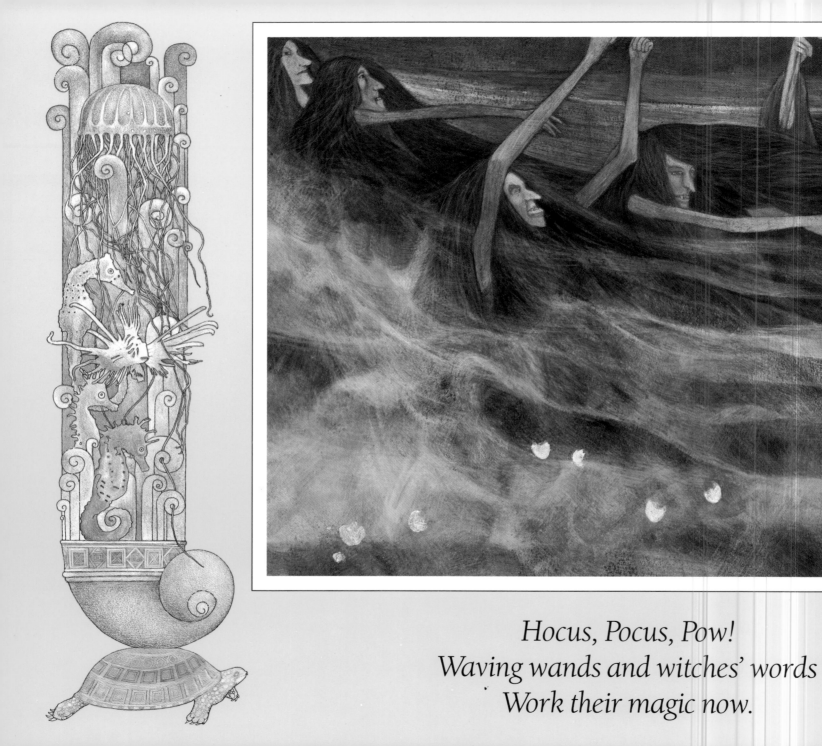

Hocus, Pocus, Pow!
Waving wands and witches' words
Work their magic now.

Shells turn into ships,
Delicate eggshell vessels,
Wretched roundabouts.

Hidden by the mist,
Seaworthy and watertight,
They head out to sea:

Wandering witches
Search the sea for sailing ships
Of honest seamen.

A ship heaves in sight!
Ahoy! On the horizon!
Unsuspecting prey.

Witches wail and howl,
Hidden in a thundercloud,
Stirring up the seas.

Whistling up the wind,
Whipping and whirling it 'round,
They gather power.

A black cloud, white edged,
Churning troubled waters white,
Gives sailors warning.

The witch-storm attacks —
Savage winds and lashing rain
From lightning-streaked clouds.

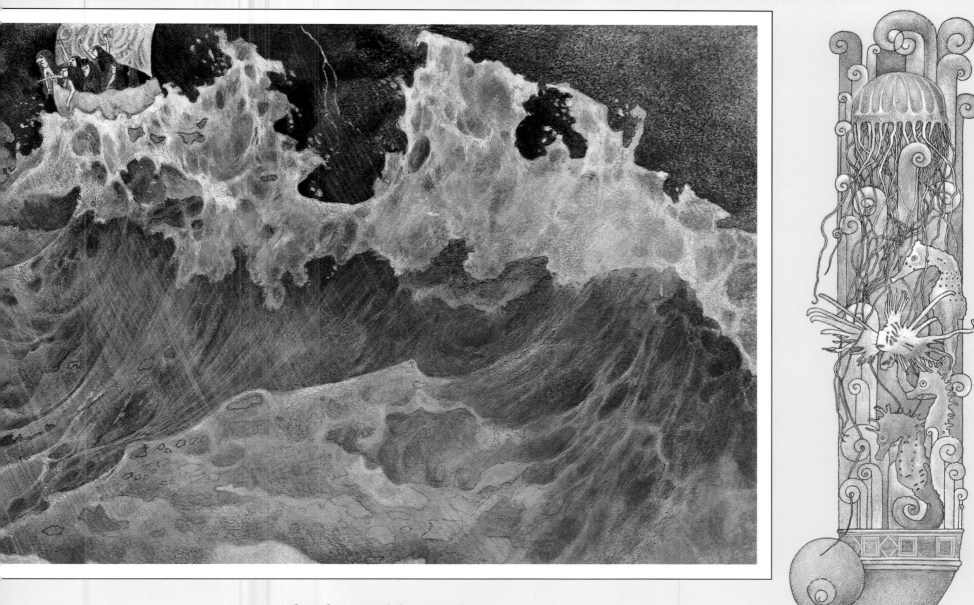

Blackened brutal seas,
Battering the bruised vessel,
Boil furiously.

Witches raise a wall
of water before the ship –
Steel sky, iron sea.

Destroying the ship,
Raging, unyielding waters
Swallow the seamen.

The drowned ship goes down
The long throat of the ocean
To cavernous depths.

Whooping and cheering,
Victorious witches watch
The watery wreck.

Escaping on brooms,
Sea witches cackle and shriek,
Their wicked work done.

Powdery remains
Of abandoned eggshell ships
Are left in their wake.

Undersea sailors,
Deep in Davey Jones' Locker
Can never go home.

Rocked in water beds,
They sleep on seashell pillows,
Dreaming of beaches."

The story's over.
But be sure to remember
Grandmother's warning:

"When you're done eating,
Give your eggshells a beating!
Never leave them whole!"

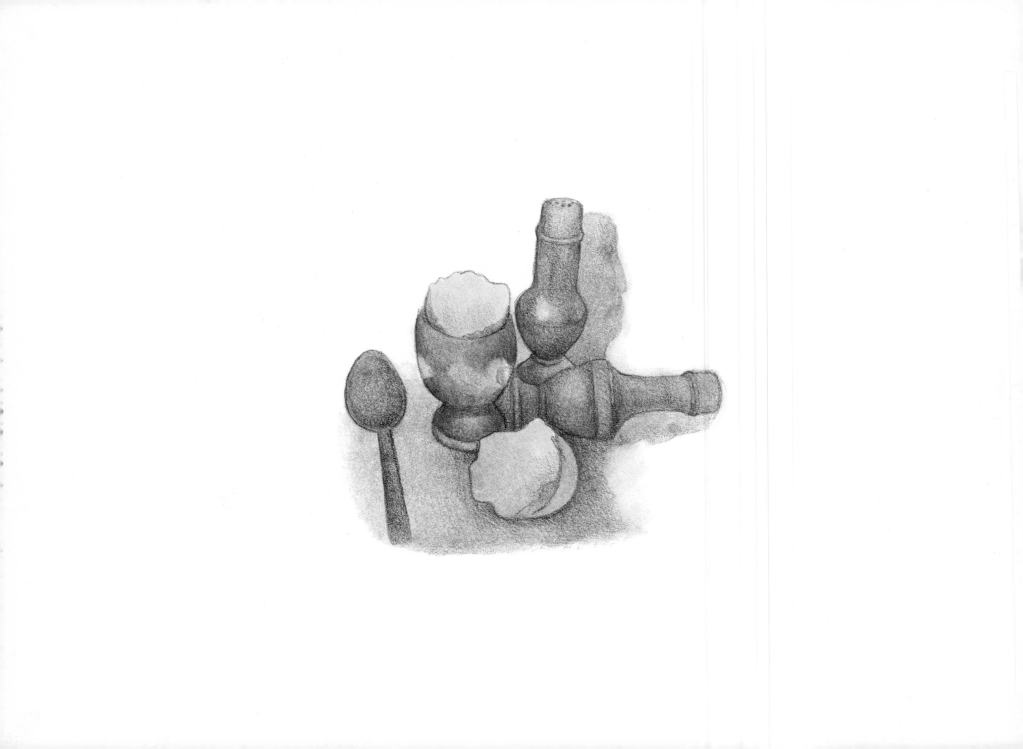